DREAMWORKS

Spirit

RIDING FREE

Lucky's Guide
to Horses & Friendship

Stacia Deutsch

L B

New York Boston

Little, Brown and Company
Hachette Book Group
1290 Avenue of the Americas, New York, NY 10104
Visit us at LBYR.com

First Edition: November 2018

Little, Brown and Company is a division of Hachette Book Group,
Inc. The Little, Brown name and logo are trademarks of
Hachette Book Group, Inc.

The publisher is not responsible for websites (or their content)
that are not owned by the publisher.

Library of Congress Control Number 2018932056

ISBNs: 978-0-316-41864-5 (pbk.)

Printed in China

APS

10 9 8 7 6 5 4 3 2 1

OFFICIAL
MARK OF
SPIRIT

This book belongs to:

_____

WELCOME TO MIRADERO!

Hi!

You look as if you're new to town, but you've come to just the right place!

I'm Lucky, and I am going to be your guide to the best town on the frontier: Miradero! It might seem small now, but it's bursting with adventure. You'll see!

But before we leave the station, I should tell you a little about myself and my family. After all, it wasn't so long ago that I was the new girl in town! First, you should know that my real name is Fortuna  Esperanza Navarro Prescott. <u>Fortuna</u> means <u>luck</u> in Spanish. That's why everyone calls me Lucky!

Even though my mom died when I was little and I never really knew her, I still feel lucky to be her daughter. She was this amazing, brave horseback rider—she even performed in the circus! She's my hero. (Dad and Aunt Cora are my heroes, too.)

I grew up with my dad and my aunt Cora in the big city. My family is in the railroad business, and my dad decided we should move to the frontier—to Miradero—to start fresh. Of course, Aunt Cora wasn't going to let us go without her, so she came along. She and I don't always see things the same way, but I can't imagine life without her. So we all hopped on the train—this was when the adventure began.

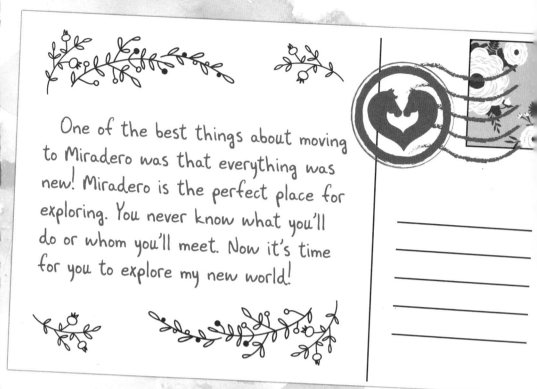

One of the best things about moving to Miradero was that everything was new! Miradero is the perfect place for exploring. You never know what you'll do or whom you'll meet. Now it's time for you to explore my new world!

Don't worry if you don't understand everything just yet. My PALs and I wrote up a glossary in the back of this book just for you! Look for words highlighted like this.

I'm going to show you the best parts of Miradero, the most amazing city on the whole frontier. I'll introduce you to my friends, and of course, we're going to hang out with Spirit, the most incredible wild mustang in the whole <u>world</u>. And after that, I'll teach you a thing or two about being the best horseback rider, just as my friends taught me.

Are you ready?

Follow me!

More About Me— Lucky!

The most important thing I can say about Miradero is that it's filled with the very best friends I've ever found. Now you're my friend, too! My dad always says that a great way to get to know a new friend is to ask him or her questions and to share about yourself. So first I'll let you know a few things about myself and then you can answer the questions below so I can learn all about <u>you</u>! What do you say?

What is your favorite subject at school?
_Reading_____

What's your favorite color?
_The light-brown color of Spirit's coat_____

What's your favorite ice cream flavor?
_Strawberry_____

What do you want to be when you grow up?
_A circus performer_____

What is something you wish for?
_More time to ride Spirit and hang out with_____
_my friends_____

What is your favorite subject at school?
_____

What's your favorite color?
_____

What's your favorite ice cream flavor?
_____

What do you want to be when you grow up?
_____

What is something you wish for?
_____
_____

Meet Spirit!

This is Spirit! He's my horse, but no one really owns him. He's a wild mustang, and when he's not having adventures with me, he's taking care of the other mustangs in his herd. Spirit's gentle and strong, super fun to be around, but sometimes stubborn. He's kind of like me! We're great partners.

When I first got to Miradero, I had never ridden a horse before. I wasn't scared, but I didn't know what to do or how to do it. I found out that there was trouble in Filbert Canyon, and I needed to warn my friends. Spirit helped me. He saved the day and Pru, Abigail, and their horses, too. That was the beginning; no one else rides Spirit now. We have this amazing bond. I help him and he helps me.

Hey, look, here come Pru and her horse, Chica Linda! Come on, I can't wait for you to meet them.

Meet Pru!

Hey, Lucky, who's your friend? It's always nice to meet someone new. You want to know about me? Hmm...let's see.

I guess the most important thing about me is that I've grown up my whole life around horses. Ask me anything, and I'll teach you the ropes, just like I taught Lucky. Oh, I love challenges, too, so make your questions hard!

When I'm not at the barn, I like to sing, but I don't perform much because I get nervous in front of people. I'm working on that, and with a little help from my friends, someday I might be brave enough to do a concert in front of a crowd!

What makes you happy?

Singing

What is your favorite food?

Licorice

Where is your favorite place to explore?

The frontier!

What is the most treasured thing you own?

Photographs of my family

What is your favorite thing to do?

Spend time with my two best friends,
Abigail and Lucky. We always find a new
adventure!

What makes you happy?

_____

What is your favorite food?

_____

Where is your favorite place to explore?

_____

What is the most treasured thing you own?

_____

What is your favorite thing to do?

_____

_____

_____

Meet Chica Linda!

You've already met Spirit, so this is my horse, Chica Linda. My palomino mare's name means <u>pretty girl</u> in Spanish, and she really is the most beautiful horse in town. And I've had her for as long as I can remember. Chica Linda never lets me down, especially not in the ring. She wins all the local competitions and has more blue ribbons than I can count. Chica Linda's amazing out on the trail, too. There's no journey too difficult for Chica Linda.

Meet Abigail!

Hey there! I'm Abigail! Wherever you find Pru and Lucky, you'll usually find me, too—unless I'm somewhere else. I like everything in Miradero—the shops, the barn, the adventures. I even like school, especially math, but also reading and writing and science and other stuff, too. I can't even think of something I don't like. I mean, well, sometimes my brother, Snips, can be super annoying. But other than that, I think I like pretty much everything. I should really think about this more. I'll let you know when I think of something.

What do you think you'll be doing when you're grown up/
finished with school?

I'll have my own bakery on Main Street.

If you could be any animal, what would you be and why?

A horse, of course. Or maybe a puppy?
Maybe a puppy riding a horse? Hard to
choose.

Who inspires you and why?

Miss Flores. She is so pretty and a really
good teacher...and I think she gets just as
annoyed with my little brother, Snips, as I
do. Smart lady.

What do you think you'll be doing when you're grown up/
finished with school?

_____

If you could be any animal, what would you be and why?

_____

_____

_____

Who inspires you and why?

_____

_____

_____

_____

Meet Boomerang!

My horse is a pinto gelding. He's loyal, super friendly, and the noblest steed in all Miradero— and probably the world! He is always willing to get muddy, play a joke, and goof around...kind of like me!

Boomerang is very talented. I've taught Boomerang to cook. I can see you don't believe me, but he really is very helpful in the kitchen. How else could I do it all? I mean, everyone wants my homemade pies and cookies—those things don't bake themselves.

I have to be careful because Boomerang isn't just the best cooking horse in town—he's the best taster, too. Sometimes he will eat the pie before it's even done.

The PALs

Aren't friends the best? I think so! Pru and Abigail are definitely the best part of Miradero. We even have a special name for ourselves: the PALs!

PALs stands for Pru, Abigail, and Lucky—three best friends. But PALs are so much more than that! We are an inseparable team. We might not agree on everything, but in the end, we support one another because that's what friends do.

Do you have your own Pru and Abigail?

Which PAL Are You Most Like?

1. While out on a ride, you see the smoke from a bonfire out in the distance. No one's supposed to go out that far. What do you do?

   A. Jump on your horse and ride as fast as you can toward the bonfire. There's sure to be <u>something</u> interesting happening out there!

   B. Consider the dangers of riding out so far and how much time is left until sunset before choosing the safest option.

   C. Nuh-uh! Seems like a bad idea...but if your PALs are in, you're not about to let them ride off on their own!

2. Spirit comes to find you and seems desperate. You understand from his neighing and nudging you forward that one of the mares from his herd is injured. What do you do?

   A. Hurry to the mare. You'll look first and figure out what to do second.

   B. Gather medical supplies from the barn and bring them to the field. You don't know what the injury is, but you feel confident you can help.

   C. Oh no! It's hard to get in close to the wild herd. You figure your calm ways might allow you to get close, but once there, you'll need your friends to help with the mare.

3. There's a rockslide that blocks the train tracks. Knowing a train is barreling down those rock-covered tracks, what do you do?

   A. Get there fast. There are people to save and a train to stop!

   B. Consider that there might be some things to take. Perhaps you'll start a warning fire? Or need a rope? Your horse can carry tools and supplies in a saddlebag, so you start packing for an emergency.

   C. Ask your friends what they think you all should do. Consider their answers and help them come to a compromise. Then, together, you will all ride like the wind to figure out a way to stop that train!

4. It's a party! Everyone in town is coming together for the Harvest Festival. You've spent extra time getting dressed and doing up your hair, when Spirit arrives with Abigail on Boomerang and Pru on Chica Linda for a quick, fun ride. What do you do?

   A. Jump on! You might get messy, but it'll be worth it.

   B. Suggest they come back later. Getting up the nerve to go to such a fancy party wasn't easy, and you don't want to chicken out now.

   C. Try to do both. Fast ride, then back for the festival. If you sit very, very still and don't make any sudden moves, you probably won't get dirty.

5. You see the flyers for a horseback competition at the barn! You can sign up for any event you'd like—which one do you choose?

A. Flag tipping, which means riding at full speed, weaving in and out of poles, tipping them over as you pass, and galloping toward the finish line.

B. Barrel racing. You go around three barrels at top speed. To do well in this competition, you need grace, form, and a lot of practice.

C. Egg-in-Spoon relay. You ride with an egg on your spoon through obstacles, pass the egg to your team of friends, and then each of them rides, too. The team that gets to the finish line first and without breaking their egg <u>wins</u>!

If you chose mostly As, you're most like Lucky! You love to be a little adventurous...and don't always think things through. But that's okay, because you know you can depend on your best PALs to have your back. You and Lucky would ride in the wildest parts of the Miradero desert with your wild stallions...and have a whole lot of fun along the way!

If you chose mostly Bs, you're most like Pru! You can think quickly on your feet, you're practical, and you're always planning a few steps ahead. Never stick your hand in a dark cave, because you don't know what's lurking inside—that's some practical Pru advice that you'd live by. You'd enjoy spending long days at the barn, helping take care of the horses and learning to be the best rider you can be!

If you chose mostly Cs, you're most like Abigail! You're fun, a little goofy, and always looking on the bright side. You might get distracted sometimes, but your ideas are always creative, and you love to make people smile. A fun day for you would be drinking hot cocoa and baking, then decorating the barn, and finally taking a sunset ride across a meadow. There would definitely be s'mores!

17

Now that you've met the PALs and gotten to know our horses, let me show you all around town. It's a small place, but there's a lot to see. Come on—you never know whom we might run into!

Frontier living is so different from city life! I thought I'd never get used to it. Miradero has only two streets. Crazy, right? Just two. I mean, in the city, we had loads of streets and loads of places to go—not just one general store, one ice cream shop, and one school. Can you believe that?

But once I got to know the frontier, I realized that we have things here that I couldn't have in the city, like horses and wild adventures and hills to climb and valleys to explore and my new friends.

I bet your hometown is just as awesome as Miradero. Before we start the tour, will you show us what your home looks like?

Your Town

Your town looks so cool!

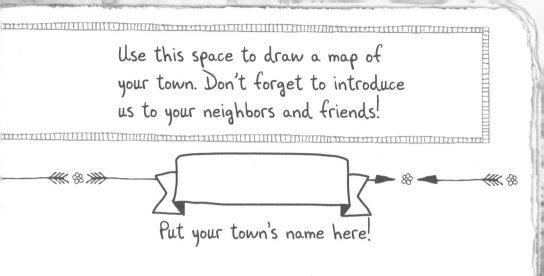

Use this space to draw a map of your town. Don't forget to introduce us to your neighbors and friends!

Put your town's name here!

Let's start our tour of Miradero at Town Hall... and look who's there: It's Maricela....

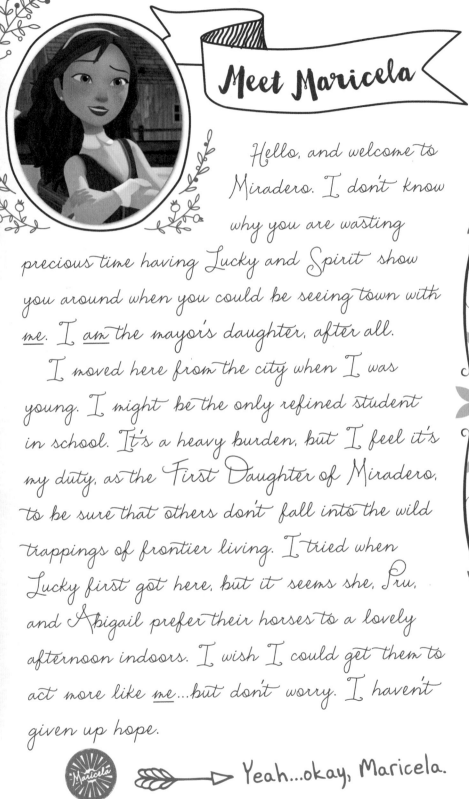

Meet Maricela

Hello, and welcome to Miradero. I don't know why you are wasting precious time having Lucky and Spirit show you around when you could be seeing town with me. I _am_ the mayor's daughter, after all.

I moved here from the city when I was young. I might be the only refined student in school. It's a heavy burden, but I feel it's my duty, as the First Daughter of Miradero, to be sure that others don't fall into the wild trappings of frontier living. I tried when Lucky first got here, but it seems she, Pru, and Abigail prefer their horses to a lovely afternoon indoors. I wish I could get them to act more like _me_...but don't worry. I haven't given up hope.

Yeah...okay, Maricela.

Lucky's House

Welcome to my house! Spirit will wait for us outside while I introduce you to my dad and Aunt Cora. Aunt Cora isn't a big fan of horses in living rooms, it turns out....

Meet Aunt Cora

Ahem, excuse me. I'd like a formal introduction to our special guest! I'm Cora, Lucky's aunt and Jim's sister. I'm here to ensure Lucky turns out polite, kind, and well-mannered...and always steps in with proper introductions. It's very nice to meet you.

Here on the frontier, away from the rest of our family, we must keep our family traditions and history close to our hearts. Lucky and I created this beautiful family tree together. Lucky, won't you share our family tree with your guest? Then, we'd all love to learn more about your roots.

Lucky's Family Tree

A family tree is a diagram of the people in your family. Family trees are awesome because no matter what kind of family you have, there's always space for the branches to grow and spread in unique ways!

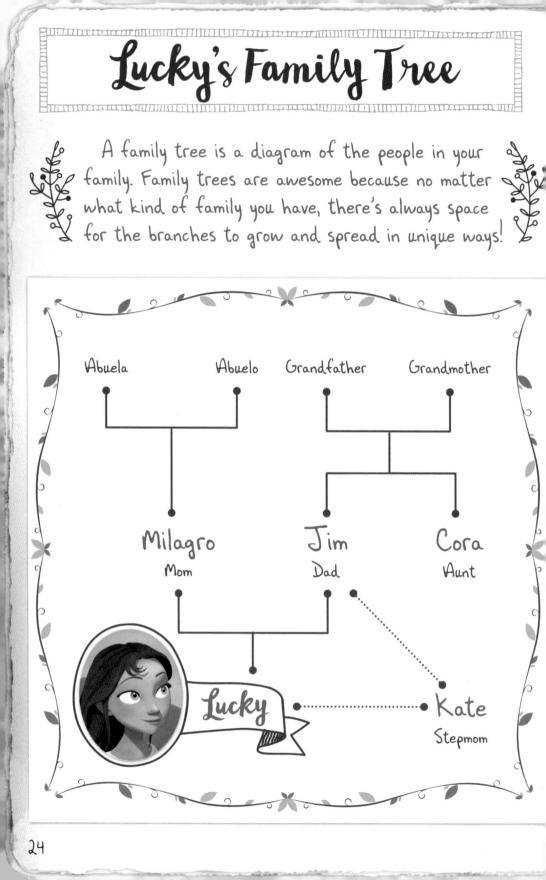

Abuela   Abuelo   Grandfather   Grandmother

Milagro
Mom

Jim
Dad

Cora
Aunt

Lucky

Kate
Stepmom

Draw Your Own Family Tree

I can't wait to learn about your family, too!

To create your own family tree, start with you on the bottom. Now let's see those branches! Ask around if you need help. You never know what interesting people, facts, or secrets you'll discover!

You

Afternoon Tea with Aunt Cora

It's time for a break. When we have guests, we welcome them with a bit of tea, properly prepared. But before we can eat, we must set the table just right. Here are the things you will need. Place them on your table in the correct positions, like so:

Water Cup

Bread Plate

Butter Knife

Teacup

Napkin

Salad Fork

Dinner Fork

Dinner Plate

Knife

Soup Spoon

Teaspoon

Now that the table is set, we are ready to enjoy our tea. That means it's time for four courses of delicious food, meant to be eaten delicately. We serve each course with a fresh pot of tea. First on the menu is soup or salad, followed by an array of finger sandwiches. After that comes my favorite part: scones served with cream and jam! And don't forget the dessert and petit fours.

Oh dear...Girls!

Abigail, stop licking the jam off your fingers.

Lucky, do not put any sugar cubes in your pockets to give to Spirit later! These are for the tea.

Pru, sip–don't guzzle.

My, my. Clearly that's enough for today.

Meet Jim

You must be Lucky's new friend! I'm so glad you came to Miradero today. Did you enjoy the train ride? I certainly hope so, since trains are my business.

As long as there have been trains, the Prescotts have been part of the rails. I'm glad we moved to Miradero to run the railway because living on the frontier is exactly the life Lucky's mom would have wanted for Lucky. I'm so proud of the young lady she's become while in Miradero. And I must say, I missed the excitement of the frontier myself. I think this is just the right place for us—and for you!

Al Granger's Ranch

Meet Al Granger

Lucky got to introduce her dad, so now let's meet mine. My dad is a wrangler with his own ramada. That means he takes care of horses here in the barn, in the ramada, and in the pasture. My dad has a tender hand whether he's breaking a wild stallion (which means domesticating a wild horse), helping birth a foal, or hooking up a cart to a team. I've learned everything about horses from him. Maybe someday I'll be a wrangler, too.

Howdy. I hear you'd like to know a bit about horse wrangling. Well, you've come to the right place.

You have to know a lot about horses to do this job.

To start, a horse has two instincts when it's afraid—to <u>run</u> or to <u>fight</u>, just like a human. A good wrangler has to move slowly, talk softly, and be careful not to startle a horse.

Wranglers make sure the horses are fed and have plenty of water, and often take care of minor wounds and injuries.

Wranglers can also be in charge of making sure the corrals are maintained and cleaned, but their main job is to look after the horses.

The most important thing my dad ever said is that if you approach a horse quietly and with love, you will make a friend for life. Right, Chica Linda?

Abigail's House

Pru's house is always great for practicing and learning more about riding, but Abigail's house always smells like fresh-baked cookies! Unfortunately, those cookies are usually being stolen by her little brother, Snips. Want to meet him, too?

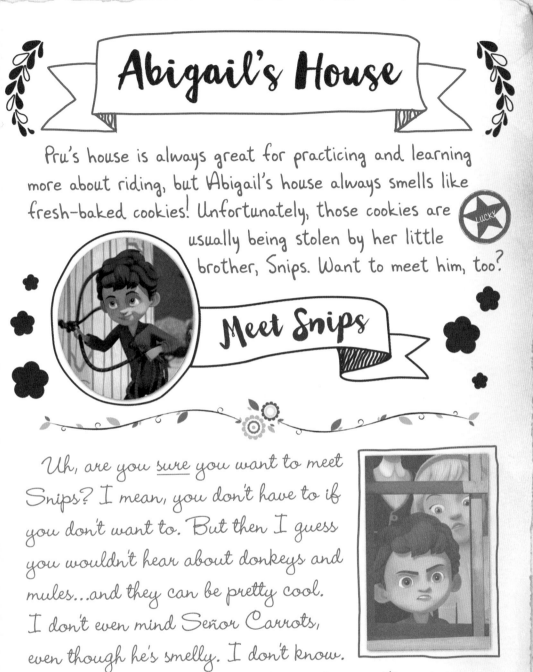

Meet Snips

Uh, are you _sure_ you want to meet Snips? I mean, you don't have to if you don't want to. But then I guess you wouldn't hear about donkeys and mules...and they can be pretty cool. I don't even mind Señor Carrots, even though he's smelly. I don't know. You can choose. Snips is my brother, so I never get to choose if I want to meet him because I already know him, and he lives in my house.

So, if you really want to meet Snips, don't forget I warned you.

Where Is Snips Hiding?

Of course, Snips is missing—again—when I actually need to find him! Good thing Lucky loves to solve a mystery, just like the heroine from her favorite book series, Boxcar Bonnie! You can help!

Where Is Snips Hiding?

"Snips! Where are you, Snips?" Abigail called out to her brother.

Abigail, Pru, and Lucky were running up to Abigail's house when Lucky skidded to a stop. "Whoa!" she exclaimed as she nearly twisted her ankle in a deep hole in the front yard. "What's that?" she asked Abigail.

"I don't know, but I bet Snips made that hole," Abigail said. "Where is he?" She burst into the house, calling her brother's name, but no one answered.

"Snips is missing," Pru said.

"This looks like a job for Boxcar Bonnie," Lucky said, pulling out a notebook and a pen. Boxcar Bonnie was her favorite detective. She'd read all the books. "What would Boxcar Bonnie do?" She paused, then realized exactly what her heroine would do. "We need to search for clues."

"I have one!" Abigail said. She had found a floppy carrot on the kitchen counter. It was rotten and not good for eating. "Eww." She threw it into the trash. "Maybe he got some fresh carrots and went to feed his donkey?"

"To the barn!" Pru announced.

"The Case of the Missing Snips. Clue number one." Lucky wrote down soggy carrots.

The PALs rushed to the barn, calling Snips's name. He wasn't there, but they did find another clue.

"Sawdust," Pru said, running her finger through the finely sifted wood shavings. "There isn't usually sawdust in the barn, just hay." Pru considered the clue.

"Sawdust," Lucky repeated, scratching her head thoughtfully. She wrote it down. "Clue number two." Then, searching around the barn, Lucky found another clue. She picked up a crinkled leaf near Señor Carrots's stall. "Autumn is almost over, and winter is coming," Lucky said. She wrote down winter as the third clue.

Lucky looked at her three clues. Then she wrote down a fourth clue: hole in Abigail's yard. "I know where Snips is," she said at last.

"Where?" Abigail and Pru asked.

"I'll show you..." Lucky said. She shut her notebook. "Come with me."

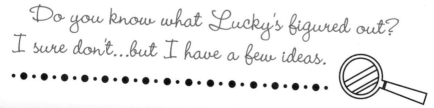

Do you know what Lucky's figured out?
I sure don't...but I have a few ideas.

<u>Theory 1</u>: Snips was in the field getting the last of the carrots. With winter coming, he wanted to make sure that he had enough carrots for his donkey to last the whole chilly season. The best way to preserve carrots on the frontier is to put them in an outdoor storage pit, cover it in sawdust, and bury them underground. The PALs helped Snips carry back his load and bury the carrots in the yard. They put a sign over the hole, marking the spot where treats were hidden for hungry donkeys...and horses, too!

<u>Theory 2</u>: Snips was in his bedroom, reading a story-book. Lucky realized that none of the clues made any sense, and Snips hadn't answered their calls because he had the door closed and couldn't hear them.

<u>Theory 3</u>: Soggy carrots, sawdust, and winter—the clues could mean only one thing: Snips was planning a party! The girls found him in the schoolhouse decorating for Señor Carrots's birthday. Sawdust on the floor. Carrots for the guests. Señor Carrots's birthday was in the winter. And the hole? Oh, that was an accident. Señor Carrots had eaten the dirt and made a hole.

Theory 1 is correct!

Schoolhouse

Here we are at the schoolhouse. My teacher is going to marry my dad... which is definitely weird, but I like the idea of a new Prescott! Miss Flores—I mean, Kate—is actually pretty cool once you give her a chance.

Meet Kate

Oh, it's so nice of you to stop by the schoolhouse. I simply love my life here in Miradero. I was raised in the Las Hermanas de Santa Cecilia Orphanage and didn't know my own parents, so I appreciate that Miradero feels like one big family.

When I grew up, I decided to become a teacher. I like when my students' eyes brighten as they learn about the solar system or dinosaur fossils or arithmetic. It almost makes up for all the times I have to chase Snips and those twins, Bianca

and Mary Pat, around my classroom. No one said this job would be easy, but when that bell rings to start the day, I am always ready for whatever challenges arise. I have a favorite class project that I'd like to share with you and Lucky.

Ooh! That sounds really cool!

How to Make an Animated Storybook!

First you need a stack of identical small pieces of paper. For my storybook, I'm going to draw a flower growing.

1) I start by drawing a stem near the edge of the paper.

2) On the next piece, I draw the same stem—but longer! Then I add leaves and petals.

3) I keep going until I've drawn the whole flower blossoming.

4) When it's done you can flip the stack of paper quickly with your thumb and watch the flower grow!

Ice Cream Parlor

Next stop on the Miradero tour: the ice cream parlor! It has the best ice cream in town.

It has the only ice cream in town.

And that makes it the best. Here comes Mr. Winthrop now.

Meet Mr. Winthrop

Oh, it's you young ladies again. I am sure your new friend is plenty nice, but I don't have time for this—or any other trouble—right now. See, I run this ice cream parlor and Winthrop's General Store. I'm Miradero's busiest entrepreneur! If you actually want some ice cream, I'll get you a scoop, but please take it outside.

Since Lucky is your guide today, let me tell you this: That girl used to work here. It was her first job.

I can help you find your first job so you can be as busy as I am one day. Just don't go opening any ice cream parlors or general stores in this area.

Mr. Winthrop's Tips for Finding a First Job

I can't hire everyone, so here are some tips to help you find that great first job.

Ask Yourself:
What kinds of things are interesting to you? I like ice cream and supplying exactly what the town needs, but that might not be for you. Do you like animals? Food? Math? Once you have an idea of what kind of job you'd like to do, it's time to do some research!

Do Research:
There are a lot of things to figure out when you're looking for a job: Who hires kids your age? How are you going to get there? How much time do you have to dedicate to your new job?

Talk to People:
It's time to hit the sidewalk. With a parent or adult, go to places you'd like to work and ask to see the owner or manager. They might be hiring, and you can learn how to apply.

Be Responsible:
Whether you get paid or just volunteer, a first job is a big responsibility, so make sure you set your alarm clock, show up on time, and be the best employee ever. (I'm not kidding; you should be the best you can be.)

LUCKY I never thought that scooping ice cream would be my first job. It was a lot more fun than I had expected. I guess, if I really thought about it, my first job could have been helping at Mr. Granger's barn or working at the railroad office for my dad...but sometimes life takes unexpected twists.

What do you think your first job might be?

_____
_____
_____
_____
_____
_____
_____
_____
_____
_____
_____
_____
_____
_____
_____
_____
_____
_____
_____
_____
_____
_____

Javier & Turo

Here we are in the town square. Hey, look, it's Javier and Turo. Let's go! You will love them!

Hey, Lucky, who's your friend? I'm Javier. Buenos días. A friend of Lucky's is a friend of mine. I'm a <u>vaquero</u>; that's Spanish for <u>cowboy</u>. I grew up on a chuck wagon, riding along with my father as we moved across the wide-open spaces. Every night, we'd sleep under the stars, and he'd tell me stories of the range. I learned everything I need to know about horses, camping, and performing for the rodeo out on the trail.

Hey, I have <u>una buena idea</u>! Come by the barn later, and I'll teach you some rope tricks. That is my specialty. See you later. <u>Hasta luego</u>, my friend.

Hello, Lucky's friend. I'm Turo. I work as the blacksmith's apprentice, making tack for the horses of town. I make saddles and horseshoes and reins—pretty much anything your horse might need. I'm still learning, but someday, I'll have my own blacksmith shop. Maybe you'll come back to Miradero for the grand opening! I could help you decide what your horse needs.

TURO

Thanks, Javier and Turo—we are off to the barn next! The tour continues....

The Barn

The barn is where your horse rests and hangs out. It also happens to be where Pru, Abigail, and I hang out, too, but you don't have to do that! Most barns have three different areas: stalls, a feed room, and a tack room. Which one do you want to see first? **LUCKY**

This is the stall. The horses need soft bedding, usually either straw or wood shavings. The bedding must be clean and dry and deep enough that they can lie down in it without getting sores from the hard ground. You must clean the stall twice a day and make sure the horse has ample clean water twice a day. **PRU**

Abigail You need a separate feed room, either in the barn or nearby, where you can store your hay and grain. Hey, Boomerang, don't eat it all!

Another room in the barn would be the tack room.... **LUCKY**

TURO Hey, Lucky, Pru, Abigail...Can I explain about tack?

Of course! I mean, Spirit doesn't even use tack, so, Turo, take it away! **LUCKY**

Turo's Tack Talk

Each item (or tack) we use on the horse makes the ride more comfortable—for the horse and the rider. Take a look at this pretty horse here. You'll see many different kinds of tack. I'll show you what a rider needs.

Getting a horse ready to ride is called "tacking up."

Saddle

Reins

Bridle

Horn

Girth

Saddle Pad

Stirrup

Part 3: Horses!

Wild vs. Domestic

First things first! It's important to remember that horses can be domestic or wild, just like Spirit! Wild horses live in a herd—that's a group of horses with one stallion and several mares, and the foals, which are the baby horses with skinny, wobbly legs. The stallion will lead the herd to grazing and water. This brave leader also protects his herd from other stallions as well as predators such as coyotes, mountain lions, wolves, and bears.

While wild horses are incredible to watch, they're not so easy to ride. I got really <u>lucky</u> with Spirit—but most people will find their special bond with domestic horses, like Chica Linda and Boomerang. Domestic horses live in a stall, corral, or pasture. These horses need human partners to bring them hay and fresh water twice a day. It's up to the human owners to protect their horses from wild predators and other dangers.

Señor Carrots and I are here to protect you, horsies!

I didn't have my own horse when I moved to Miradero. In fact, I'd never ridden. I dreamed about horses, though. I always wondered what it would be like to ride. My dream horse was way different from the real one I found when I met Spirit.

Now you can use this stencil to draw your very own dream horse! You can draw it right here or on a sheet of paper and cut it out. Don't forget to name it!

LUCKY

Decorate Your Own Stable Stall!

Spirit doesn't like to be in the barn much, but he still has his own stall for whenever he wants to stop by. If you had a horse of your own, how would you decorate the stable?

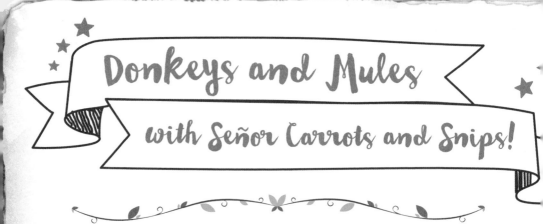

Ahem! Excuse me, Lucky! I'm going to be the guide now.

Today, I am going to teach you about donkeys. That's right, Miss Flores, watch out 'cause Snips is here, and soon I'll be teaching at the schoolhouse and you'll be...doing other stuff.

First thing to know—don't ever confuse a donkey with a pony. It's insulting. **Donkeys are way better. Here is Señor Carrots, Best Donkey in the Universe.**

We will now compare my donkey to my sister's horse to see which is better.

Horses are smart, but not smarter than Señor Carrots. I'll tell you why. Horses like to work hard. See? That's not very smart at all!

Donkeys don't need very much food, which means leftovers for me.

Horses eat everything.

The evidence is clear: Donkeys win. Horses lose.

Now, let us check out a mule. That means he's a mix-up of a donkey and a horse. But donkeys are *still better*.

Now, to end our lesson, here's a quiz:

What is the greatest animal in the whole world?

Answer: A DONKEY!

Finding Your Perfect Horse

Let's start with what's comfortable for you: Do you like riding on a light, thin saddle or a heavy, thick one with a horn?

Light and thin

Heavy and thick

Do you want to ride fast or slow?

Do you want to ride trails, exploring the outdoors?

Fast

Slow

Yes

No

Do you want to jump over poles, logs, and streams?

Your perfect breed is an Appaloosa!

Perhaps you'd like a bicycle instead of a horse?

Yes

No

Your perfect horse is a Mustang!

Do you want to go to shows and win ribbons?

Yes

No

Okay, then, one more question.

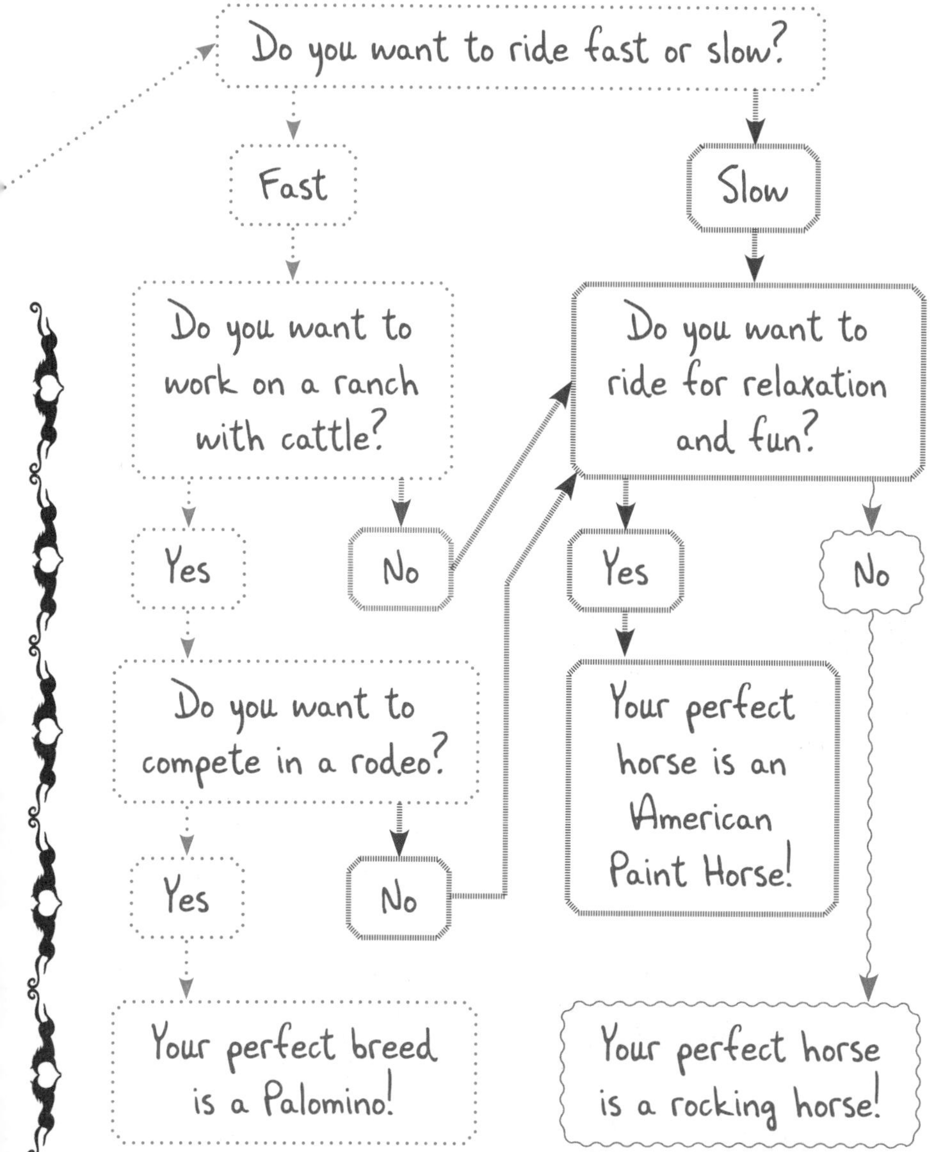

Do you want to ride fast or slow?

Fast

Slow

Do you want to work on a ranch with cattle?

Do you want to ride for relaxation and fun?

Yes

No

Yes

No

Do you want to compete in a rodeo?

Your perfect horse is an American Paint Horse!

Yes

No

Your perfect breed is a Palomino!

Your perfect horse is a rocking horse!

(I ride without a saddle, so if that's what you like, your horse is a wild Mustang, and you can turn the page.)

♘ Name the Parts of the Horse ♘

Here's a horse. Here's a list of parts. Can you label this handsome guy with the correct parts?

Crest   Hoof   Knee
Dock   Muzzle   Shoulder
Tail   Flank   Barrel

1. _____

2. _____

3. _____

4. _____

5. _____

6. _____

7. _____

8. _____

9. _____

1.Crest, 2. Muzzle, 3. Flank, 4.Dock, 5. Tail, 6. Shoulder, 7. Barrel, 8. Knee, 9.Hoof

Decorate with Horseshoes

Don't forget the fun part! Decorating the barn. No one's more passionate about decorating than—

ME! Decorating! Yay! Where should we start? First rule, nothing should be too low or close to the horses. I mean, Boomerang has a stomach of steel and can eat pretty much anything, but other horses aren't as fortunate. I have an idea...let's use old horseshoes!

53

I'll ask Turo for one, but you can use these. If you have a metal horseshoe lying around the house or at a barn nearby, you can paint it. You can decorate these.

There's one super-duper important thing to know: When you hang a horseshoe, the open side has to go up. If it's upside down, the luck runs out, right down the wall! No one wants that. So to keep your luck in the shoe, make sure you hang it like the letter U! Then you'll have luck, even if your name isn't Lucky!

Check out the super-fancy decorated horseshoe I made for Boomerang's stall!

Abigail

freedom
love
adventure

PALs Horse Treats

You're a quick learner. But you haven't learned everything just yet...like just how much horses love treats. Spirit's always stealing my snacks, so sometimes it's

smarter to bring him his own.

And I know that Chica Linda loves sugar cubes! Did you know you can make your own?

If you don't have a horse, you can put sugar cubes in tea. (A nice gift for Aunt Cora, maybe?)

Always ask a parent for help before you cook or bake! The kitchen can get a little...messy.

Chica Linda's Favorite Sugar Cubes

What You'll Need:

¼ cup sugar

½ teaspoon water

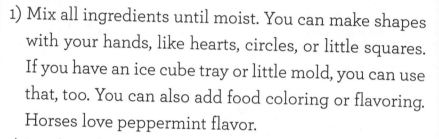

What to Do:

1) Mix all ingredients until moist. You can make shapes with your hands, like hearts, circles, or little squares. If you have an ice cube tray or little mold, you can use that, too. You can also add food coloring or flavoring. Horses love peppermint flavor.

2) Let the cubes sit overnight until they harden.

3) Rush to the barn. You'll be the most popular person there!

Yum! But Boomerang has more discerning taste. He needs something a little fancier than just sugar. Horses love bananas, apples, carrots, molasses, watermelon rinds, peppermint, bread crusts, hardened salt (called a <u>lick</u>), dried berries, and oats. In my kitchen, we can make a super-duper healthy horse snack! And it's so healthy that you can eat it, too!

I mean, if you want to...

Abigail's No-More-Stinky-Breath Horse and Human Cookies

What You'll Need:

1 cup rolled oats

¼ cup water

1 to 2 tbsp. molasses

5 peppermint candies

What to Do:

1) Mix the oats and water until the oats are damp.
2) Add molasses by the tablespoon until the mixture is sticky.
3) Roll into balls and press a peppermint in the middle of each cookie.
4) Put in refrigerator (uncovered) to harden.

Boomerang! Spit that out right now. The cookies aren't ready yet!

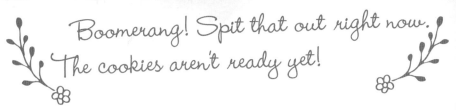

Part 4: Riding!

The PALs are here to introduce you to riding! We have some easy questions. You might not know the answers yet, but I bet you can guess! And once you know these three things, you'll be ready to start riding.

Horseback Riding Basics with the PALs:

Pru's Question:

It's important to get to know your horse before you ride. What are the best ways to show your horse you want to be friends?

A. give him an apple
B. pet him gently
C. scratch his neck
D. kiss his nose
E. all the things above

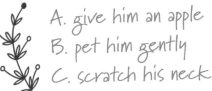

Abigail's Question:

Grooming is my favorite part. Can you match the grooming tool with how to use it?

1. lead rope

2. dandy brush

3. currycomb

4. hoof-pick

5. soft brush

A) This brush is good for the horse's face and around the eyes.

B) This round brush removes dirt and mud from your messy horse. (Boomerang is always messy.)

C) Use this to tie the horse to a post so it doesn't run away while you groom.

D) This hard brush is used after the currycomb to get off the dirt.

E) Cleaning the muck from the bottom of your horse's feet is important.

Lucky's Question:

Let's get dressed for a ride.
Which of these things do you need?

    A. long pants
    B. a cute skirt
    C. close-toe shoes like boots
    D. a helmet
    E. mittens

Solutions:

Pru's Question: E

Abigail's Question: 1-C, 2-D, 3-B, 4-E, 5-A

Lucky's Question: A, C, and D

Draw Your Own Saddle!

Spirit doesn't like a saddle, but other horses understand their humans need saddles to ride! Did you know you can decorate your saddle? Trace this one and make it reflect your horse's personality! Once you're done, you can cut it out for your horse to wear!

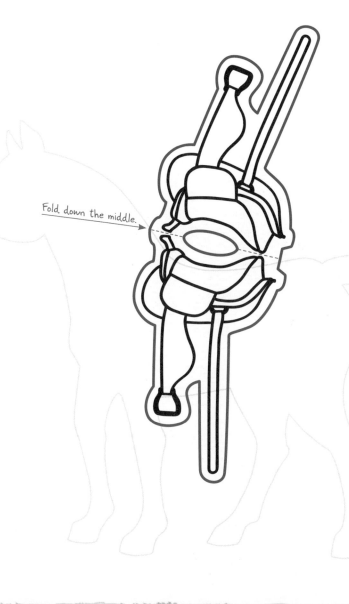

Fold down the middle.

Create Your Own Course!

I like designing jumping courses for competition. Horses can jump one fence at a time or up to three! Pop out the fences, hay bales, and barrels, and prop them on the bases to create your own course, then draw arrows to show the rider which way to go. When you're done, you can try it out with the horse you drew earlier. I know Chica Linda and I can't wait to try for the best time!

Competition Riding with Pru

Now that you know all about horses, let's go to the ramada. It's a fenced ring where we can ride!

LUCKY

If you want to learn about competitive riding, you came to the right PAL. My dad taught me everything there is to know about riding in a competition. You see, there are two main categories of competitive riding in the western world: English and Western.
Let me break it down:

PRU

<u>English competition</u> isn't what we do every day on the ranch, but I love it! I have to have a special saddle to ride. It's called an English saddle, and it's lightweight, so the rider sits very close to the horse and has a lot of control. The reins are connected, and you hold them in two hands. When I'm in my English saddle, Chica Linda and I can jump both in the arena and out in a field, an event called cross-country.

There are two English competitions that I really enjoy:

<u>Dressage</u> is a French word that means "training," and in Europe most young horses start off in dressage and move to jumping afterward. Dressage is all about obedience and precision. The four ways a horse can move are called gaits: from a slow walk to faster a trot, an even faster canter, and finally a gallop.

<u>Eventing</u> is a horse competition that requires a horse to participate in three events: dressage; show jumping in an area; and cross-country jumping over natural obstacles like hedges, logs, and ditches, or into water.

A <u>Western saddle</u> has a horn that a rope lasso can be
tied to or wrapped around. It's a much heavier saddle
and designed to withstand the tug-of-war between a
horse and a steer. There are two separate reins that
the rider holds in one hand. In competition, Chica
Linda and I have to do all the things a cowboy would do
on the range. In the rodeo competition, there are calf
roping, bulldogging, and barrel racing events.

Gymkhana and O-Mok-See are super-fun competitions
in which games are played on horseback, like riding
fast and knocking down poles, racing while the rider
has to balance an egg in a spoon, and riding around
big barrels.

★ Design Your Own Blue Ribbon ★

Huh, you're getting pretty good. Looks as if I might have some competition out there. That's fine, as long as your name isn't Maricela.

You've earned this blue ribbon for sure!

Staying Fashionable

Wow! You're learning fast. Pru, is there anything else to know about dressage?

Dressage is very traditional, and can be really strict—in a good way! Everything has its place...right down to the clothing you should wear.

If you must ride a horse, why not look your best? Tell me more, Pru.

Well, you'll need white pants, a black belt, and these tall black boots that go above your knees. They're called Spanish-cut riding boots.

 I love long boots. <u>Very chic.</u>

Okay, then, you'd also want a white shirt, wide stock tie, white gloves, and a black safety helmet.

I've heard that you can fancy up your outfit by adding gems or gold thread or pins to your belt or wearing a cute pin with your tie. Dressage outfits are adorable for wearing around town, too!

You can't dress up if you aren't going to compete on horseback.

Who's going to stop me?   I am—

Come on, Pru. It's pointless to argue with her. Instead, let's show Maricela what you can do in the ring. She might look good, but she can't win a blue ribbon if she doesn't ride.

True...

I think I'll go decorate my helmet.

Draw Your Own Riding Gear

I am going to design my own outfit for walking around. No smelly horses are going to dirty it up. What will you design?

Horse Badges

We've done so much today. Before it's over, I think you deserve some badges.

Badges! Yay! Do I get some, too?

LIVE Freely

Riding FREE

Anyone can earn badges. Think about what we've learned today, answer the questions, and earn the badges. Check your answers throughout the book!

Trick Riding with Javier

Ah, amigos, I am so glad to see you here in the riding ring. I love trick riding here. Trick riding was originally created in battle. Ancient warrior horsemen used to stand on horseback, shoot arrows from a galloping horse,  hang from one side to avoid being hit, and even mount and dismount while moving fast. Members of Native American tribes did similar stunts on their ponies while riding bareback. It's very exciting and scary to watch; that's because trick riding is extremely dangerous. Only very advanced riders and professionals, like me, should try these tricks.

Lucky has been practicing on Spirit. Lucky's mother was a trick rider, so it's in her blood. She falls off Spirit's back a lot, but she gets right up again.

All that practice means she'll be an expert in no time. I'd better watch out. I might not be the best trick rider in Miradero much longer if I don't keep my eye on her!

<u>Ándale</u>, and off we go!

Fun and Games with Abigail!

Sometimes, we PALs just want to play around with our horses. Abigail always has a goofy game ready to play. What are we up to today, Abigail?

Bubbles and paint and messiness and cleanliness! Boomerang loves it when I paint him! I make swirls and handprints. Sometimes I get fancy and paint a beautiful sunset, but he gets impatient with how long that takes and tries to bite my nose.

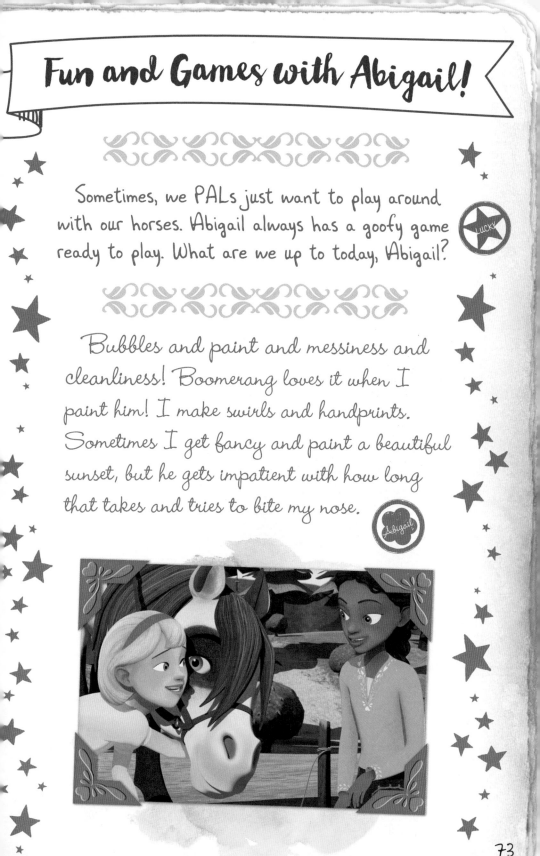

After painting (or riding or anything messy), I like to give Boomerang a bubble bath. All I need is a little shampoo and some water, and suds away! He isn't picky about the shampoo, but if it smells like cinnamon, mint, lemons, or food, he'll eat the bubbles. Boomerang smells so good after a bath!

Once he's all clean and shiny, I like to braid Boomerang's mane and tail. I use ribbons for decoration, but I have to be careful because Señor Carrots likes to eat Boomerang's ribbons!

There you go, Boomerang. Not all fun is in the riding ring. Tonight, we'll go on a trail ride.

Horse Jokes with Snips

A trail ride! Oh boy! Señor Carrots and I can do a comedy routine at the campfire. We're very funny, and all it'll cost you is one nickel! <u>You don't have a nickel?</u> Okay, since you're new to town, special price. <u>It's free.</u> Don't say anythin', but when Abigail comes to the show, I'm gonna tell her it costs a dime.

What does it mean if you find a horseshoe?
Some poor horse is walking around in his socks!

Where do horses go if they are sick?
The <u>horse</u>pital!

What's a horse's favorite state?
<u>Neigh</u>braska!

Which side of the horse has more hair?
The outside!

What did the mommy horse say to her baby?
It's pasture bedtime!

What do you call a horse that lives next door?
A <u>neigh</u>bor!

Part 5: Frontier Fillies

Sorry, Snips. Tonight's trail ride is for the Frontier Fillies! It's our scouting club!

Ah, shucks. Come on, Señor Carrots. We know when we aren't welcome.

Frontier Fillies have a lot of fun! We go spelunking, rock climbing, and white water rafting, and sing songs. We have a jamboree, and best of all—

Fillies go camping! Hanging out under the stars, sleeping on the ground, telling ghost stories, and having big adventures all on our own. And this time, you're coming with us.

And, boy, are you in for a treat! Because it's craft time!

Frontier Fillies Fun

Craft time is the best time! Let's make some cool stuff for bird watching. Just don't forget to ask a parent for help before you get started.

Abigail

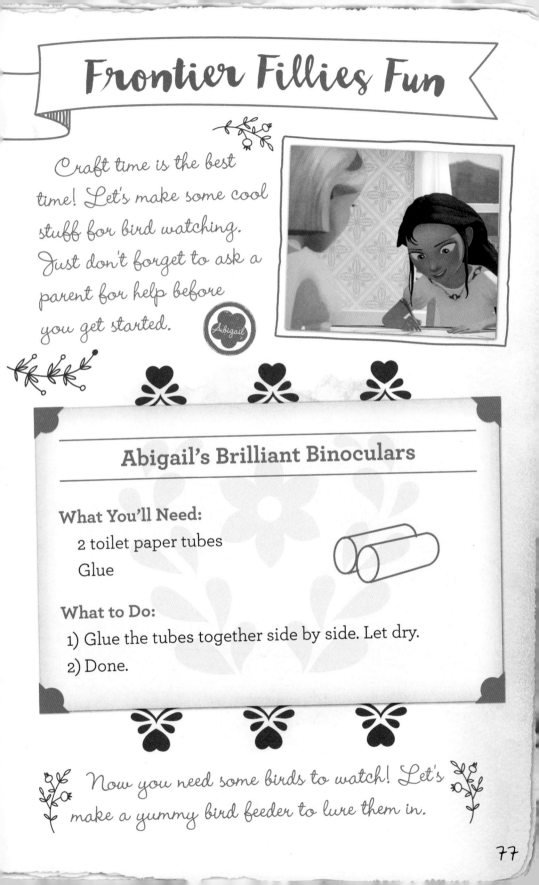

Abigail's Brilliant Binoculars

What You'll Need:
- 2 toilet paper tubes
- Glue

What to Do:
1) Glue the tubes together side by side. Let dry.
2) Done.

Now you need some birds to watch! Let's make a yummy bird feeder to lure them in.

Peanut Butter Bird Feeder
(For Birdie Consumption ONLY)

What You'll Need:

A large pinecone
Peanut butter
A plastic knife
Birdseed
String for hanging

What to Do:

1) Find a pinecone. Pick a pretty one; birds like big, fat pinecones.

2) Use your knife to spread peanut butter all over the pinecone, and then let Boomerang lick your fingers. (Okay, that's what I do...but if you don't have a horse, you can lick your own fingers.)

3) Roll the pinecone in birdseed to cover the peanut butter. (Don't lick your fingers again, unless you like birdseed!)

4) Hang your bird feeder from a tree, high enough that your horse—or Snips—can't reach it!

Sassy Sit-Upon

What You'll Need:

    Two large 12" x 12" squares of fabric
    Needle and thread
    Newspaper or magazine or old mail
      or any paper trash

What to Do:

1) Thread the needle and tie a knot in the string.
2) Poke the needle through one corner of the two fabrics and pull till the knot is tight. Then about ¼ inch down the side, stick it back in through the fabric in the other direction. Pull through.
3) Poke up through the fabric again, and down again, and up again...until three of the four sides are sewn together. It should look like a pillowcase.
4) Stuff the newspaper into the open side.
5) Sew it closed.

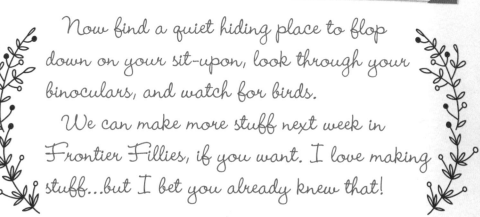

Now find a quiet hiding place to flop down on your sit-upon, look through your binoculars, and watch for birds.

    We can make more stuff next week in Frontier Fillies, if you want. I love making stuff...but I bet you already knew that!

The Frontier Fillies are all about traditions. I have a really cool one to share with you. These are called Ojo de Dios. They are a Native American craft, and are known to be a little magical. The God's Eye sees things that human eyes don't, so be careful!

Ojo de Dios

What You'll Need:

Two sticks of the same length

Yarn

Scissors

What to Do:

1) Tie two twigs together in the middle.
2) Start wrapping yarn around Arm One then go around Arm Two, around Arm Three and Arm Four, and keep going. If that color yarn runs out, tie it to the twig and start a new color.
3) At the end make a loop so you can hang it in your room or in your horse's stall!

To make a blazing campfire, we'll need dry wood and matches, and rocks for a protective fire circle—

The wood is wet. I forgot to bring the matches. There aren't rocks around. What should we do?

I know! Let's make a different kind of campfire. The kind you can eat. I know, you're thinking: How can we eat a fire? Is this some kind of secret Miradero magic? Nope. Anyone can eat a delicious fire. I'll show you how:

Edible Campfires

What You'll Need:

Pretzel sticks   Candy corn   Chocolate candies

What to Do:

1) Start with a fire circle of chocolate candies.
2) Make a teepee with the pretzel sticks, as you would with logs or wooden sticks if you were making a real campfire.
3) Tuck candy corn under the pretzel sticks to look like fire.
4) Show everyone that you can "eat fire." Yum.

Abigail and Snips's Famous S'mores

Go away, Snips. You're not a Frontier Filly.

Okay, I'll just take my bag here of marshmallows, graham crackers, and chocolate, and go home.

Wait! How about you can be a Frontier Fellow, but just for today...if you share.

Yay! I'm gonna be a Frontier Fellow, cooking up some Frontier Fun.

Snips's S'mores

Take a marshmallow. Stuff it down on the top of a long clean stick. Hold it over the fire until the marshmallow is toasted on the outside and squishy inside. Oh boy. Don't eat it yet, no matter how much you might want to. Then, take two crunchy graham crackers and a big piece of chocolate. Make a sandwich. Crackers on the outside, chocolate and mushy marshmallow inside. Wait a second....DON'T EAT IT YET! Peek under a cracker, and you can add banana slices, sprinkles, nuts, cherries, more nuts, more chocolate....AUGH! I CAN'T HOLD BACK ANY MORE!!!! I GOTTA EAT IT!

Now let's do that all over again.

Story Time for Lucky and Spirit's Greatest Adventure

Frontier Fillies like to hang out by the campfire, and do you know what the best part of a campfire is?

S'mores! I was just thinking about how delicious they are....

S'mores are great, but I was thinking storytelling.

Stories are good, but not very delicious. Do you have a story for us, Lucky?

I do! Fill in the blanks with the right kind of word, and then tell the story. You can do this one again and again!

Once, when Lucky and Spirit were heading home after

a long ride, Lucky saw a(n) _____ shadow. Spirit
(adjective)

_____ and took _____ steps
(past tense verb)   (number)

forward, but then reared back.

"It's just a trick of the _____ sun," Lucky
(color)

assured Spirit. The _____ shadow was blocking
(adjective)

the way to Miradero.

Lucky could see Spirit was looking _____
(direction)

for another route, but the _____ branches were
(adjective)

thick and covered with thorns on both sides of the path.

"We can't turn around," Lucky said. "_____
(place)

is that way."

The _____ shadow grew bigger, and
(adjective)

Lucky was determined to face it bravely.

"Come on," Lucky told Spirit, edging him _____.
(direction)

"Let's go home."

Suddenly the shadow shifted and a(n) _____
(adjective)

ghost stepped out onto the pathway. It was huge! The

ghost had _____ and _____, with
(plural noun)   (plural noun)

long _____. Suddenly there was another
(plural body part)

ghost blocking the pathway! This one was the same size

as the first, but it was moaning _____ and
(sound)

_____.
(another sound)

Lucky screamed!

Spirit bucked.

Lucky held on tightly.

The ghosts _____.
(past tense verb)

Both Pru and Abigail threw off sheets that were so

_____ they covered the girls, plus their horses.
(adjective)

"We _____ you!" Pru chuckled.
(past tense verb)

Spirit snorted. He acted as if he hadn't been fooled.

"We knew it was you all along," Lucky said, rolling her

eyes. "There are no ghosts in the _____."
(place)

Just then, they all heard a strange sound nearby. It was

like a _____. The PALs all looked at one
(sound)

another. None of them had made that noise. They were

really _____!
(past tense verb)

The horses took them back to Miradero, as fast as they

could!

How to Write Supersecret Codes!

As Frontier Fillies, we PALs do a lot of important work—and sometimes that means we need to write secret messages. Did you know it's easy to create secret codes only you and your PALs can understand? The trick is to mix up the letters in the alphabet, or even make up a brand-new symbol to represent a letter! All you have to do is write a key that you and your friends can use to decode the messages.

 You can use codes to keep certain little brothers out of your business!

Señor Carrots and I are master code breakers. It might take days or even years, but we'll break that code someday. You can't trick us.

Can you crack my secret code below?

Code: L'v cezsdeuu zao ab bae'u kbaaz tbdo ve yznw.

Here's the key I would normally share only with Pru and Abigail, but I think we can trust you to keep it a secret! Please don't show Snips.

A	B	C	D	E	F	G
Z	Y	N	O	E	C	K

H	I	J	K	L	M	N
T	L	I	W	D	V	A

O	P	Q	R	S	T	U
B	X	M	S	U	F	G

V	W	X	Y	Z
P	J	R	Q	H

I'm fearless and no one's gonna hold me back.

Campfire Stories

I love telling stories by the campfire!
Here are some fun ideas to get started.
I can't wait to read what you write.

Abigail

The PALs were out on a trail ride. Boomerang stumbled over a rock and twisted his ankle. He'll be fine in a few days, but Abigail can't ride him home. What do the PALs do now?

Close your eyes and imagine there is a horse next to you. Now write a description with all the details.

Lucky is waiting for Spirit to meet her after school, but he doesn't show up. She gets Pru and Abigail to go with her to look for him. Where do they go first? Second? Where do they finally find him?

Lucky, Abigail, and Pru are out for a short trail ride when it begins to rain. At first they think it's just a light rain, so they keep going, until suddenly, the thunder booms and the lightning flashes, and they know they need a place to wait for the storm to pass. Where do they go, and what do they do to pass the time?

Spirit finds a lost foal in the woods. He brings the baby horse to Lucky, who knows they need to return the foal to her mother. Pru and Abigail want to help. What do the PALs do to help the baby, and where do they find the mother?

Now write your own story here!

_____
_____
_____
_____
_____
_____
_____
_____
_____
_____
_____
_____
_____
_____
_____
_____
_____
_____
_____
_____
_____
_____

How to Volunteer to Help Horses Near You!

Remember when we were talking about getting a job? Sometimes it's really nice to work somewhere and not expect to be paid. Volunteering is working from your heart. And if I were going to volunteer, it would be with horses, of course!

Check out these cool ideas! If you were going to volunteer, which one would you like the most? Rank them 1-4 on the next page.

Become a Counselor

You could be a counselor for kids at a horse camp. This would mean helping kids all day with the horses, but also with other activities like lunch and games.

Feed & Groom

I know a terrific place that rescues horses and rehabilitates them. There are places like this in almost every town. Here, you'd feed and groom horses to help out. *Jim*

Competitions

I like to volunteer at competitions. Help is always needed to hand out ribbons, check the scores, and make sure that everyone competing is happy! *PRU*

Horse Rides

I know a barn that gives horse rides for the disabled. You could help answer questions in the office and help where needed in the ramada. *Abigail*

Rankings

1. _____
2. _____
3. _____
4. _____

Farewell for Now!

Well, we're back at the train station. I hope you enjoyed your visit to Miradero. Spirit and I loved showing you around town. We hope you will spend some time at a stable near you and think of us every time you ride! Come back and see us soon!

Your PALs forever!

Glossary

Bonfire: A large controlled outdoor fire

Breaking: Training a horse so it may be ridden with a saddle

Canter: A three-beat horse gait that is faster than a trot and slower than a gallop

Corral: A closed pen for livestock

Foal: A young horse

Frontier: The land outside a developed territory

Gait: A horse's foot movements

Gallop: A fast movement during which all four of a horse's feet are off the ground in a smooth stride

Gelding: A castrated (neutered) male horse

Gymkhana and O-Mok-See: Horse competitions with races and fun games for riders of all ages

Herd: A group of wild horses that live together

Horn: The pommel on the front of Western saddles

Jamboree: A festive gathering

Mare: An adult female horse

Molasses: A sweet syrup that is separated from sugar in manufacturing

Pasture: Land used for grazing

Ramada: A fenced ring in which a person can ride

Ring: A closed riding arena, either outside or inside

Tack: The equipment or accessories used to ride a horse

Trot: A gait in which the horse walks while alternately lifting each diagonal pair of legs